Parents and teachers love
Magic Tree House books, too!

I am the mother of four young sons who are thoroughly enjoying the adventures of Jack and Annie! We eagerly await each new release! We also use your books as Christmas and birthday gifts for friends and cousins—a welcome gift for the children and their parents!—C. Anders

We overheard the children in the schoolyard talking and laughing about "special friends." Upon further investigation, those friends turned out to be none other than Jack and Annie. These children have become devoted fans of your books. As parents, it is inspiring to see our children so absorbed in books.
—M. Knepper and P. Contessa

The library soon will have a new addition— something that I have dreamed of for a long time—a real wooden Magic Tree House and a beautiful tree mural to accompany it. . . . There are many Magic Tree House experts in every class. It's wonderful to see their enthusiasm and their eagerness to read the books.—R. Locke

MAGIC TREE HOUSE® #3

Mummies in the Morning

by Mary Pope Osborne

illustrated by Sal Murdocca

A STEPPING STONE BOOK™

Random House 🏠 New York

For Patrick Robbins, who loves ancient Egypt

Text copyright © 1993 by Mary Pope Osborne.
Illustrations copyright © 1993 by Sal Murdocca.
All rights reserved under International and Pan-American
Copyright Conventions. Published in the United States by
Random House, Inc., New York, and simultaneously in Canada
by Random House of Canada Limited, Toronto.

Library of Congress Cataloging-in-Publication Data
Osborne, Mary Pope. Mummies in the morning /
by Mary Pope Osborne ; illustrated by Sal Murdocca.   p.   cm. —
(The magic tree house series ; #3) "A First Stepping Stone book."
SUMMARY: Jack and his younger sister take a trip in their tree house
back to ancient Egypt, where they help a queen's mummy continue her
voyage to the Next Life.
ISBN 978-0-679-82424-4 (trade)—ISBN 978-0-679-92424-1 (lib. bdg.)
[1. Time travel—Fiction.   2. Mummies—Fiction.
3. Magic—Fiction.   4. Tree houses—Fiction.]
I. Title.   II. Series: Osborne, Mary Pope. Tree house series ; #3.
PZ7.O81167Mr 1993 [Fic]—dc20 92-50665
Printed in the United States of America
60 59 58 57 56 55 54 53 52 51 50 49 48

Random House   New York, Toronto, London, Sydney, Auckland

Contents

Mummies
in the Morning

1

Meow!

"It's still here," said Jack.

"It looks empty," said Annie.

Jack and his seven-year-old sister gazed up at a very tall oak tree. At the top of the tree was a tree house.

Late-morning sunlight lit the woods. It was almost time for lunch.

"Shhh!" said Jack. "What was that noise?"

"What noise?"

"I heard a noise," Jack said. He looked around. "It sounded like someone coughing."

"I didn't hear anything," said Annie. "Come on. Let's go up."

She grabbed onto the rope ladder and started climbing.

Jack tiptoed over to a clump of bushes. He pushed aside a small branch.

"Hello?" he said. "Anybody there?"

There was no answer.

"Come on!" Annie called down. "The tree house looks the same as it did yesterday."

Jack still felt that someone was nearby. Could it be the person who'd put all the books in the tree house?

"Ja-ack!"

Jack gazed over the top of the bushes.

Was the mysterious person watching him now? The person whose name began with M?

Maybe M wanted the gold medallion back. The one Jack had found on their dinosaur adventure. Maybe M wanted the leather bookmark back. The one from the castle book.

There was an M on the medallion. And an M on the bookmark. But what did M stand for?

"Tomorrow I'll bring everything back," Jack said loudly.

A breeze swept through the woods. The leaves rattled.

"Come on!" called Annie.

Jack went back to the big oak tree. He grabbed onto the rope ladder and climbed up.

At the top he crawled through a hole in the wooden floor. He tossed down his backpack and pushed his glasses into place.

"Hmmm. Which book is it going to be today?" said Annie.

She was looking at the books scattered around the tree house.

Annie picked up the book about castles.

"Hey, this isn't wet anymore," she said.

"Let me see."

Jack took the book from her. He was amazed. It looked fine. Yesterday it had gotten soaked in a castle moat.

The castle book had taken Jack and Annie back to the time of knights.

Jack silently thanked the mysterious knight who had rescued them.

"Watch out!" warned Annie.

She waved a dinosaur book in Jack's face.

"Put that away," said Jack.

The day before yesterday the dinosaur book had taken them to the time of dinosaurs.

Jack silently thanked the Pteranodon who had saved him from a Tyrannosaurus rex.

Annie put the dinosaur book back with the other books. Then she gasped.

"Wow," she whispered. "Look at *this*."

She held up a book about ancient Egypt.

Jack caught his breath. He took the book from her. A green silk bookmark stuck out of it.

Jack turned to the page with the bookmark. There was a picture of a pyramid.

Going toward the pyramid was a long parade. Four huge cows with horns were pulling a sled. On the sled was a long gold box. Many Egyptians were walking behind the sled. At the end of the parade was a sleek black cat.

"Let's go there," whispered Annie. "Now."

"Wait," said Jack. He wanted to study the book a bit more.

"Pyramids, Jack," said Annie. "You love pyramids."

It was true. Pyramids *were* high on his list

of favorite things. After knights. But before dinosaurs. *Way* before dinosaurs.

He didn't have to worry about being eaten by a pyramid.

"Okay," he said. "But hold the Pennsylvania book. In case we want to come right back here."

Annie found the book with the picture of their hometown in it. Frog Creek, Pennsylvania.

Then Jack pointed to the pyramid picture in the Egypt book. He cleared his throat and said, "I wish we could go to this place."

"*Meow!*"

"What was *that*?" Jack looked out the tree house window.

A black cat was perched on a branch. Right outside the window. The cat was staring at Jack and Annie.

It was the strangest cat Jack had ever seen. He was very sleek and dark. With bright yellow eyes. And a wide gold collar.

"It's the cat in the Egypt book," whispered Annie.

Just then the wind started to blow. The leaves began to shake.

"Here we go!" cried Annie.

The wind whistled louder. The leaves shook harder.

Jack closed his eyes as the tree house started to spin.

It spun faster and faster! And faster!

Suddenly everything was still.

Absolutely still.

Not a sound. Not a whisper.

Jack opened his eyes.

Hot bright sunlight nearly blinded him.

"*Me-ow!*"

2

Oh, Man. Mummies!

Jack and Annie looked out the window.

The tree house was perched on the top of a palm tree. The tree stood with other palm trees. A patch of green surrounded by a sandy desert.

"Meow!"

Jack and Annie looked down.

The black cat was sitting at the base of the tree. His yellow eyes were staring up at Jack and Annie.

"Hi!" Annie shouted.

"Shhh," said Jack. "Someone might hear you."

"In the middle of the desert?" said Annie.

The black cat stood and began walking around the tree.

"Come back!" Annie called. She leaned out the window to see where the cat was going.

"Oh, wow!" she said. "Look, Jack."

Jack leaned forward and looked down.

The cat was running away from the palm trees. Toward a giant pyramid in the desert.

A parade was going toward the pyramid. The same parade as in the Egypt book.

"It's the picture from the book!" said Jack.

"What are those people doing?" asked Annie.

Jack looked down at the Egypt book. He read the words under the picture:

When a royal person died, a grand funeral procession took place. Family, servants, and mourners followed the coffin. The coffin was called a sarcophagus. It was pulled on a sled by four oxen.

"It's an Egyptian funeral," said Jack. "The box is called a sar...sar...sar...oh, forget it."

He looked out the window again.

Oxen, sled, Egyptians, black cat. All were moving in a slow, dreamy way.

"I'd better make some notes about this," said Jack.

He reached into his backpack and pulled out his notebook. Jack always kept notes.

"Wait," said Jack. And he wrote:

Coffin called Sarcophagus

"We'd better hurry," said Annie, "if we want to see the mummy."

She started down the rope ladder.

Jack looked up from his notebook.

"Mummy?" he said.

"There's probably a mummy in that gold box," Annie called up. "We're in ancient Egypt. Remember?"

Jack loved mummies. He put down his pencil.

"Good-bye, Jack!" called Annie.

"Wait!" Jack called.

"Mummies!" Annie shouted.

"Oh, man," said Jack weakly. "Mummies!" She sure knew how to get to him.

Jack shoved his notebook and the Egypt book into his pack. Then he started down the ladder.

When he got to the ground, he and Annie took off across the sand.

But as they ran a strange thing happened.

The closer they got to the parade, the harder it was to see it.

Then suddenly it was gone. The strange parade had disappeared. Vanished.

But the great stone pyramid was still there. Towering above them.

Panting, Jack looked around.

What had happened? Where were the people? The oxen? The gold box? The cat?

"They're gone," said Annie.

"Where did they go?" said Jack.

14

"Maybe they were ghosts," said Annie.

"Don't be silly. There's no such thing as ghosts," said Jack. "It must have been a mirage."

"A what?"

"Mirage. It happens in the desert all the time," said Jack. "It looks like something's there. But it just turns out to be the sunlight reflecting through heat."

"How could sunlight look like people, a mummy box, and a bunch of cows?" said Annie.

Jack frowned.

"Ghosts," she said.

"No way," said Jack.

"Look!" Annie pointed at the pyramid. Near the base was the sleek black cat.

He was standing alone. He was staring at Jack and Annie.

"*He*'s no mirage," said Annie.

The cat started to slink away. He walked along the base of the pyramid and slid around a corner.

"Where's he going?" said Jack.

"Let's find out," said Annie.

They dashed around the corner—just in time to see the cat disappear through a hole in the pyramid.

3

It's Alive!

"Where did he go?" said Jack.

He and Annie peeked through the hole.

They saw a long hallway. Burning torches lit the walls. Dark shadows loomed.

"Let's go in," said Annie.

"Wait," said Jack.

He pulled out the Egypt book and turned to the section on pyramids.

He read the caption aloud:

> Pyramids were sometimes called Houses of the Dead. They were nearly all solid stone, except for the burial chambers deep inside.

"Wow. Let's go there. To the burial chambers," said Annie. "I bet a mummy's there."

Jack took a deep breath.

Then he stepped out of the hot, bright sunlight into the cool, dark pyramid.

The hallway was silent.

Floor, ceiling, walls—everything was stone.

The floor slanted up from where they stood.

"We have to go farther inside," said Annie.

"Right," said Jack. "But stay close behind me. Don't talk. Don't—"

"Go! Just go!" said Annie. She gave him a little push.

Jack started up the slanting floor of the hallway.

Where was the cat?

The hallway went on and on.

"Wait," said Jack. "I want to look at the book."

He opened the Egypt book again. He held it below a torch on the wall. The book showed a picture of the inside of the pyramid.

"The burial chamber is in the middle of the pyramid. See?" Jack said. He pointed to the picture. "It seems to be straight ahead."

Jack tucked the book under his arm. Then they headed deeper into the pyramid.

Soon the floor became flat. The air felt different. Musty and stale.

Jack opened the book again. "I think we're almost at the burial chamber. See the picture? The hallway slants up. Then it gets flat. Then you come to the chamber. See, look—"

"*Eee-eee!*" A strange cry shot through the pyramid.

Jack dropped the Egypt book.

Out of the shadows flew a white figure.
It swooshed toward them!
A mummy!
"It's alive!" Annie shouted.

4

Back from the Dead

Jack pulled Annie down.

The white figure moved swiftly past them. Then disappeared into the shadows.

"A mummy," said Annie. "Back from the dead!"

"F-forget it," stammered Jack. "Mummies aren't alive." He picked up the Egypt book.

"What's this?" said Annie. She lifted something from the floor. "Look. The mummy dropped this thing."

It was a gold stick. About a foot long. A dog's head was carved on one end.

"It looks like a scepter," said Jack.

"What's that?" asked Annie.

"It's a thing kings and queens carry," said Jack. "It means they have power over the people."

"Come back, mummy!" Annie called. "We found your scepter. Come back! We want to help you!"

"Shush!" said Jack. "Are you nuts?"

"But the mummy—"

"That was no mummy," said Jack. "It was a person. A real person."

"What kind of person would be inside a pyramid?" asked Annie.

"I don't know," said Jack. "Maybe the book can help us."

He flipped through the book. At last he found a picture of a person in a pyramid. He read:

Tomb robbers often carried off the
treasure buried with mummies.
False passages were sometimes
built to stop the robbers.

Jack closed the book.

"No live mummy," he said. "Just a tomb
robber."

"Yikes. A tomb robber?" said Annie.

"Yeah, a robber who steals stuff from
tombs."

"But what if the robber comes back," said
Annie. "We'd better leave."

"Right," said Jack. "But first I want to
write something down."

He put the Egypt book into his pack. He
pulled out his notebook and pencil.

He started writing in his notebook:

tomb robber

"Jack—" said Annie.

"Just a second," said Jack. He kept writing:

Tomb robber tried to steal

"Jack! Look!" said Annie.

Jack felt a whoosh of cold air. He looked up. A wave of terror went through him.

Another figure was moving slowly toward them.

It wasn't a tomb robber.

No. It was a lady. A beautiful Egyptian lady.

She wore flowers in her black hair. Her long white dress had many tiny pleats. Her gold jewelry glittered.

"Here, Jack," Annie whispered. "Give her this." She handed him the gold scepter.

The lady stopped in front of them.

Jack held out the scepter. His hand was trembling.

He gasped. The scepter passed right through the lady's hand.

She was made of air.

5

The Ghost-Queen

"A ghost," Annie whispered.

But Jack could only stare in horror.

The ghost began to speak. She spoke in a hollow, echoing voice.

"I am Hutepi," she said. "Queen of the Nile. Is it true that you have come to help me?"

"Yes," said Annie.

Jack still couldn't speak.

"For a thousand years," said the ghost-queen, "I have waited for help."

Jack's heart was pounding so hard he

thought he might faint.

"Someone must find my Book of the Dead," she said. "I need it to go on to the Next Life."

"Why do you need the Book of the Dead?" asked Annie. She didn't sound scared at all.

"It will tell me the magic spells I need to get through the Underworld," said the ghost-queen.

"The Underworld?" said Annie.

"Before I journey on to the Next Life, I must pass through the horrors of the Under-world."

"What kinds of horrors?" Annie asked.

"Poisonous snakes," said the ghost-queen. "Lakes of fire. Monsters. Demons."

"Oh." Annie stepped closer to Jack.

"My brother hid the Book of the Dead. So tomb robbers would not steal it," said the ghost-queen. "Then he carved this secret message on the wall, telling me how to find it."

She pointed to the wall.

Jack was still in shock. He couldn't move.

"Where?" asked Annie. "Here?" She squinted at the wall. "What do these tiny pictures mean?"

The ghost-queen smiled sadly. "Alas, my brother forgot my strange problem. I cannot

see clearly that which is close to my eyes. I have not been able to read his message for a thousand years."

"Oh, that's not a strange problem," said Annie. "Jack can't see anything either. That's why he wears glasses."

The ghost-queen stared in wonder at Jack.

"Jack, lend her your glasses," said Annie.

Jack took his glasses off his nose. He held them out to the ghost-queen.

She backed away from him. "I fear I cannot wear your glasses, Jack," she said. "I am made of air."

"Oh. I forgot," said Annie.

"But perhaps you will describe the hieroglyphs on these walls," said the ghost-queen.

"Hi-row-who?" said Annie.

"Hieroglyphs!" said Jack, finally finding his voice. "It's the ancient Egyptian way of writing. It's like writing with pictures."

The ghost-queen smiled at him. "Thank you, Jack," she said.

Jack smiled back at her. He put his glasses on. Then he stepped toward the wall and took a good long look.

"Oh, man," he whispered.

6

The Writing on the Wall

Jack and Annie squinted at the pyramid wall.

A series of tiny pictures were carved into the stone.

"There are four pictures here," Jack told the ghost-queen.

"Describe them to me, Jack. One at a time, please," she said.

Jack studied the first picture.

"Okay," he said. "The first one is like this."
He made a zigzag in the air with his finger.

"Like stairs?" asked the ghost-queen.

"Yes, stairs!" said Jack. "Just like stairs."

She nodded.

Easy enough.

Jack studied the second picture.

"The second one has a long box on the bottom," he said. He drew it in the air.

The ghost-queen looked puzzled.

"With three things on top. Like this," said Annie. She drew squiggly lines in the air.

The ghost-queen still seemed puzzled.

"Like a hat," said Jack.

"Hat?" said the ghost-queen.

"No. More like a boat," said Annie.

"Boat?" said the ghost-queen. She got excited. "Boat?"

Jack took another look at the wall.

"Yes. It could be a boat," he said.

The ghost-queen looked very happy. She smiled.

"Yes. Of course," she said.

Jack and Annie studied the next picture.

"The third one is like a thing that holds flowers," said Annie.

"Or a thing that holds water," said Jack.

"Like a jug?" asked the ghost-queen.

"Exactly," said Jack.

"Yes. A jug," said Annie.

Jack and Annie studied the last picture.

"And the last one looks like a pole that droops," said Annie.

"Like a curved stick," said Jack. "But one side is shorter than the other."

The ghost-queen looked puzzled.

"Wait," said Jack. "I'll draw it in my notebook. Big! So you can see it."

Jack put down the scepter and got out his pencil. He drew the hieroglyph.

"A folded cloth," said the ghost-queen.

"Well, not really," said Jack. He studied his drawing.

"But that is the hieroglyph for a folded cloth," said the ghost-queen.

"Well, okay," said Jack.

He looked at the fourth hieroglyph again. He still couldn't see the folded cloth. Unless it was like a towel hanging over a bathroom rod.

"So that's all of them," said Annie. She pointed at each picture. "Stairs. Boat. Jug. Folded cloth."

Jack wrote the words in his notebook.

stairs = 🔲   jug = 🫗

boat = 🛶   cloth = ?

"So what does the message mean?" he asked the ghost-queen.

"Come," she said. She held out her hand. "Come to my burial chambers."

And she floated away.

7

The Scroll

Jack put the scepter and his notebook and pencil into his pack.

He and Annie followed the ghost-queen. Deeper into the pyramid. Until they came to some stairs.

"The STAIRS!" said Jack and Annie.

The ghost-queen floated up the stairs.

Jack and Annie followed.

The ghost-queen floated right through a wooden door.

Jack and Annie pushed on the door. It opened slowly.

They stepped into a cold, drafty room.

The ghost-queen was nowhere in sight.

Dim torchlight lit the huge room. It had a very high ceiling. On one side was a pile of tables, chairs, and musical instruments.

On the other side of the room was a small wooden boat.

"The BOAT!" said Jack.

"What's it doing inside Queen Hutepi's pyramid?" asked Annie.

"Maybe it's supposed to carry her to the Next Life," said Jack.

He and Annie went over to the boat. They looked inside it.

The boat was filled with many things. Gold plates. Painted cups. Jeweled goblets. Woven baskets. Jewelry with blue stones. Small wooden statues.

"Look!" said Jack.

He reached into the boat and lifted out a clay jug.

"The JUG!" said Annie.

Jack looked inside the jug.

"Something's in here," he said.

"What is it?" asked Annie.

Jack felt down inside the jug.

"It feels like a big napkin," he said.

"The FOLDED CLOTH!" said Annie.

Jack reached into the jug and pulled out the folded cloth. It was wrapped around an ancient-looking scroll.

Jack slowly unrolled the scroll.

It was covered with wonderful hiero-glyphs.

"The Book of the Dead!" whispered Annie. "We found it. We found her book."

"Oh, man." Jack traced his finger over the scroll. It felt like very old paper.

"Queen Hutepi!" called Annie. "We have it! We found your Book of the Dead!"

Silence.

"Queen Hutepi!"

Then another door on the other side of the chamber creaked open.

"In there," said Annie. "Maybe she's in there."

Jack's heart was pounding. Cold air was coming through the open doorway.

"Come on," said Annie.

"Wait—"

"No," said Annie. "She's waited a thousand years for her book. Don't make her wait anymore."

Jack put the ancient scroll into his backpack. Then he and Annie slowly started to cross the drafty room.

They came to the open door. Annie went through first.

"Hurry, Jack!" she said.

Jack stepped into the other room.

It was nearly bare. Except for a long gold

box. The box was open. The cover was on the floor.

"Queen Hutepi?" called Annie.

Silence.

"We found it," said Annie. "Your Book of the Dead."

There was still no sign of the ghost-queen.

The gold box glowed.

Jack could barely breathe. "Let's leave the scroll on the floor. And go," he said.

"No. I think we should leave it in there," said Annie. She pointed to the gold box.

"No," said Jack.

"Don't be afraid," said Annie. "Come on."

Annie took Jack by the arm. They walked together. Across the room. To the glowing gold box.

They stopped in front of the box. And they peered inside.

8

The Mummy

A real mummy.

Bandages were still wrapped around the bald skull. But most of the bandages had come off the face.

It was Hutepi. Queen of the Nile.

Her broken teeth were showing. Her little wrinkled ears. Her squashed nose. Her withered flesh. Her hollow eye sockets.

Plus the rotting bandages on her body were coming off. You could see bones.

"Oh, gross!" cried Annie. "Let's go!"

"No," said Jack. "It's interesting."

"Forget it!" said Annie. She started out of the room.

"Wait, Annie."

"Come on, Jack. Hurry!" cried Annie. She was standing by the door.

Jack pulled out the Egypt book and flipped to a picture of a mummy. He read aloud:

> Ancient Egyptians tried to protect the body so it would last forever. First it was dried out with salt.

"Ugh, stop!" said Annie.

"Listen," said Jack. He kept reading:

> Next it was covered with oil. Then it was wrapped tightly in bandages. The brain was removed by—

"Yuck! Stop!" cried Annie. "Good-bye!" She dashed out of the room.

45

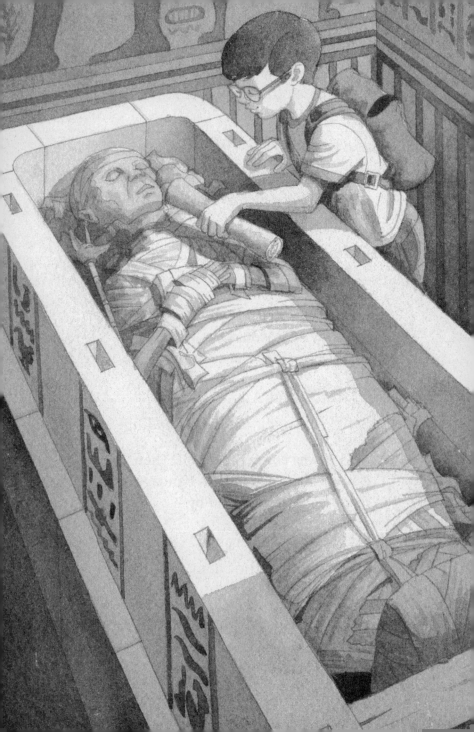

"Annie!" called Jack. "We have to give her the Book of the Dead!"

But Annie was gone.

Jack reached into his pack. He pulled out the scroll and the scepter. He put them next to the mummy's skull.

Was it just his imagination? Or did a deep sigh seem to shudder throughout the room? Did the mummy's face grow calmer?

Jack held his breath as he backed away. Out of the mummy room. Out of the boat room. Down the stairs.

At the bottom of the stairs, he heaved his own sigh. A sigh of relief.

He looked down the hallway. It was empty.

"Hey! Where are you?" he said.

No answer.

Where in the world was Annie?

Jack started down the hallway.

"Annie!" he called.

Had she run out of the pyramid? Was she already outside?

"Annie!"

"Help, Jack!" came a cry. The voice sounded far away.

It was Annie! Where was she?

"Help, Jack!"

"Annie!"

Jack started to run. Along the shadowy hallway.

"Help, Jack!" Her cry seemed fainter.

Jack stopped.

He was running *away* from her voice.

"Annie!" he called. He went back toward the burial chambers.

"Jack!"

There! Her voice was louder.

"Jack!"

Even louder!

Jack climbed the stairs. He went back into the boat room.

He looked around the room. At the furniture. The musical instruments. The boat.

Then he saw it. Another door! Right next to the door he had just come through.

The other door was open.

Jack dashed through it. He found himself at the top of some stairs.

They were just like the stairs in the other hallway.

He went down into the hallway. It was lit by torches on the wall.

It was just like the other hallway.

"Annie!" he called.

"Jack!"

"Annie!"

"Jack!"

She was running through the hallway toward him.

She crashed into him.

"I was lost!" she cried.

"I think this is one of those false passages. Built to fool the tomb robbers," said Jack.

"A false passage?" said Annie, panting.

"Yeah, it looks just like the right hallway," said Jack. "We have to go back into the boat room. And out the right door."

Just then they heard a creaking noise.

Jack and Annie turned around. They looked up the stairs.

Then they watched in horror as the door slowly creaked shut.

A deep sound rumbled in the distance. And all the torches went out.

9

Follow the Leader

It was pitch dark.

"What happened?" asked Annie.

"I don't know. Something weird," said Jack. "We have to get out of here fast. Push against the door."

"Good idea," said Annie in a small voice.

They felt their way through the darkness. To the top of the stairs.

"Don't worry. Everything's going to be okay," said Jack. He was trying to stay calm.

"Of course," said Annie.

They leaned against the wooden door and pushed.

It wouldn't budge.

They pushed harder.

No use.

Jack took a deep breath. It was getting harder to breathe. And harder to stay calm.

"What can we do?" asked Annie.

"Just . . . just rest a moment," said Jack, panting.

His heart was pounding as he tried to see through the darkness.

"Maybe we should start down the hall," he said. "Maybe we'll eventually come to . . . to an exit."

He wasn't sure about that. But they had no choice.

"Come on," he said. "Feel the wall."

Jack felt the stone wall as he climbed slowly down the stairs. Annie followed.

Jack started down the dark hallway. It

was impossible to see anything.

But he kept going. Taking one step at a time. Moving his hands along the wall.

He went around a corner. He went around another corner. He came to some stairs. He went up.

There was a door. He pushed against it. Annie pushed, too. This door wouldn't budge either.

Was this the same door they had started at?

It was no use. They were trapped.

Annie took his hand in the dark. She squeezed it.

They stood together at the top of the stairs. Listening to the silence.

"*Meow.*"

"Oh, man," Jack whispered.

"He's back!" said Annie.

"*Meow.*"

"Follow him!" cried Jack. "He's going away from us."

They started down the dark hallway. Following the cat's meow.

Hands against the wall, Jack and Annie stumbled through the darkness.

"*Meow.*"

They followed the sound. All the way through the winding hallway. Down, down, down.

Around one corner, then another. And another . . .

Finally they saw a light at the end of the tunnel. They rushed forward—out into the bright sunlight.

"Yay!" Annie shouted.

But Jack was thinking.

"Annie," he said. "How did we get out of the false passage?"

"The cat," said Annie.

"But how could the cat do it?" asked Jack.

"Magic," said Annie.

Jack frowned. "But—"

"Look!" said Annie. She pointed.

The cat was bounding away. Over the sand.

"Thank you!" called Annie.

"Thanks!" Jack shouted at the cat.

His black tail waved.

Then he disappeared in the shimmering waves of heat.

Jack looked toward the palm trees. At the top of one sat the tree house. Like a bird's nest.

"Time to go home," Jack said.

He and Annie set off for the palm trees. It was a long hot walk back.

At last Annie grabbed onto the rope ladder. Then Jack.

Once they were inside the tree house, Jack reached for the book about Pennsylvania.

Just then he heard a rumbling sound. The same sound they had heard in the pyramid.

"Look!" Annie said, pointing out the window.

57

Jack looked.

A boat was beside the pyramid. It was gliding over the sand. Like a boat sailing over the sea.

Then it faded away. Into the distance.

Was it just a mirage?

Or was the ghost-queen finally on her way to the Next Life?

"Home, Jack," whispered Annie.

Jack opened the Pennsylvania book.

He pointed to the picture of Frog Creek.

"I wish we could go home," he said.

The wind began to blow.

The leaves began to shake.

The wind blew harder. It whistled louder.

The tree house started to spin.

It spun faster and faster.

Then everything was still.

Absolutely silent.

10

Another Clue

Late-morning sunlight shone through the tree house window. Shadows danced on the walls and ceiling.

Jack took a deep breath. He was lying on the floor of the tree house.

"I wonder what Mom's making for lunch," said Annie. She was looking out the window.

Jack smiled. Lunch. Mom. Home. It all sounded so real. So calm and safe.

"I hope it's peanut butter and jelly sandwiches," he said.

He closed his eyes. The wood floor felt cool.

"Boy, this place is a mess," said Annie. "We'd better make it neater. In case M comes back."

Jack had almost forgotten about M.

Would they ever meet the mysterious M? The person who seemed to own all the books in the tree house?

"Let's put the Egypt book on the bottom of the pile," said Annie.

"Good idea," said Jack. He needed a rest before he visited any more ancient tombs.

"Let's put the dinosaur book on top of the Egypt book," said Annie.

"Yeah, good," said Jack. And a *long* rest before he visited another Tyrannosaurus rex.

"The castle book can go on the very top of the pile," said Annie.

Jack nodded and smiled. He liked thinking about the knight on the cover of the castle book. He felt as if the knight were his friend.

"Jack," said Annie. "Look!"

Jack opened his eyes. She was pointing at the wooden floor.

"What is it?" he asked.

"You have to see for yourself."

Jack groaned as he got up. He stood next to Annie and looked at the floor. He didn't see anything.

"Turn your head a little," said Annie. "You have to catch the light just right."

Jack tipped his head to one side. Something was shining on the floor.

He tipped his head a bit more. A letter came into focus.

The letter M! It shimmered in the sunlight.

This proved the tree house belonged to M.

Absolutely for sure. No question. No doubt about it.

Jack touched the M with his finger. His skin tingled.

Just then the leaves trembled. The wind picked up.

"Let's go down now," he said.

Jack grabbed his backpack. Then he and Annie climbed down the ladder.

As they stood on the ground below the tree house, Jack heard a sound in the bushes.

"Who's there?" he called.

The woods grew still.

"I'm going to bring the medallion back soon," Jack said loudly. "And the bookmark, too. Both of them. Tomorrow!"

"Who are you talking to?" asked Annie.

"I feel like M is nearby," Jack whispered.

Annie's eyes grew wide. "Should we look

for him?"

But just then their mother's voice came from the distance. "Ja-ack! An-nie!"

Jack and Annie looked around at the trees. Then they looked at each other.

"Tomorrow," they said together.

And they took off, running out of the woods.

They ran down their street.

They ran across their yard.

They ran into their house.

They ran into their kitchen.

They ran right into their mom.

She was making peanut butter and jelly sandwiches.

Guess what?

Jack and Annie may be
onstage near you sometime soon!

For more information about tickets and the show
MAGIC TREE HOUSE: THE MUSICAL
(including how to order the CD!),
visit www.mthmusical.com.

Discover the facts
behind the fiction with the

MAGIC TREE HOUSE®
RESEARCH GUIDES

The must-have, all-true companions for your favorite Magic Tree House® adventures!